Can't Catch Me!

Michael Foreman

Andersen Press
London

"Goodnight, Little Monkey," said Mum.
"Sweet dreams."

"No! It's too early for bed,"
said Little Monkey . . .

"Can't catch ME!"

"RRRROAR!
ARRrOOO!

Coming to get you and when we do . . ."

"Can't catch ME!"

"GRRRRRR!

GARRRRRROOO!
Coming to get you and when we do . . ."

"Can't catch ME!"

"HRRRRUMF!

HARRRROOO!

Coming to get you and when we do . . ."

"Can't catch ME!"

"Can't catch ME!"

"Can't Catch ME . . ."

"Can't catch ME!"

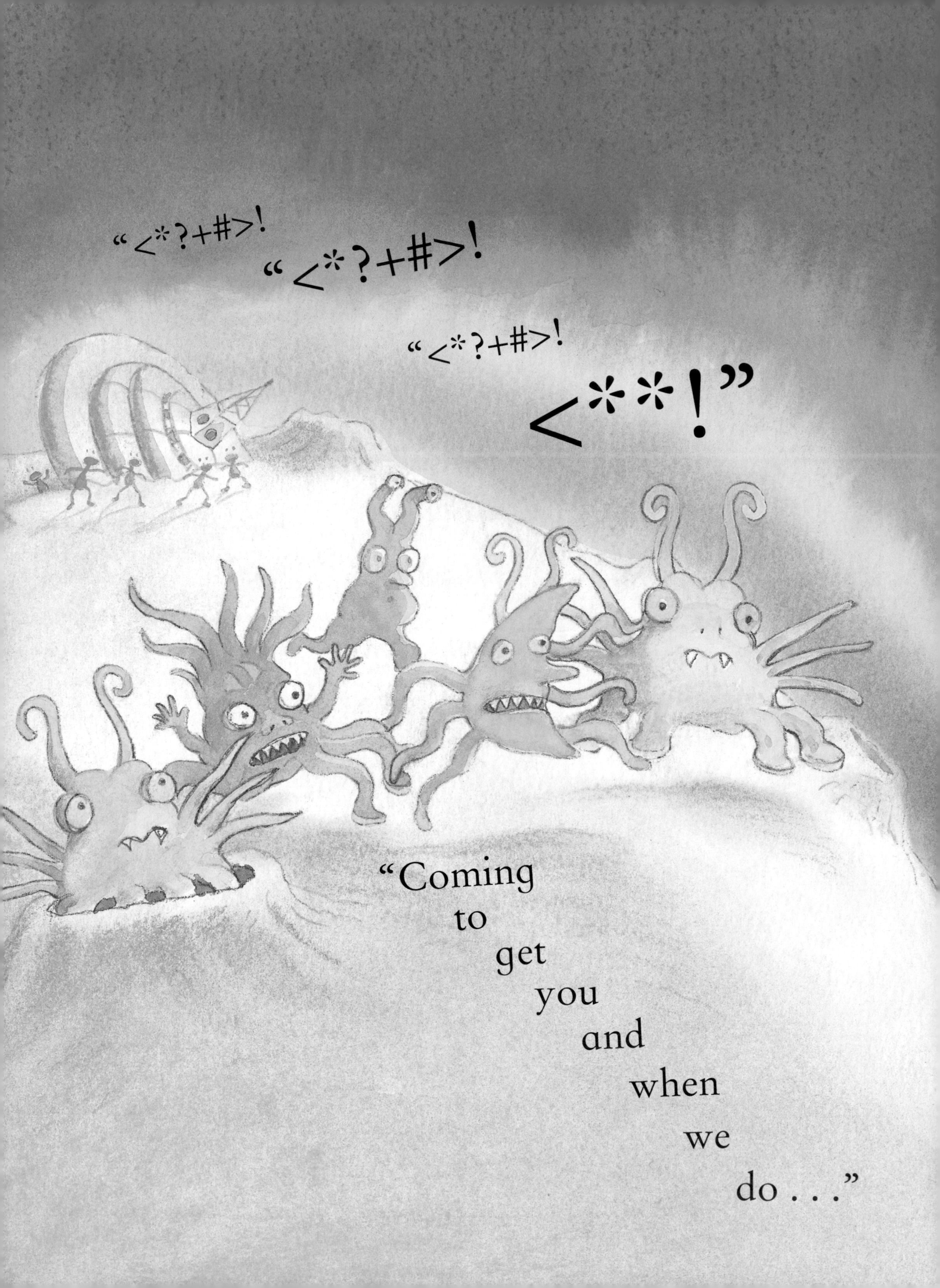

“<*?+#>!

“<*?+#>!

“<*?+#>!

<**!”

“Coming to get you and when we do . . .”

"Can't catch . . .

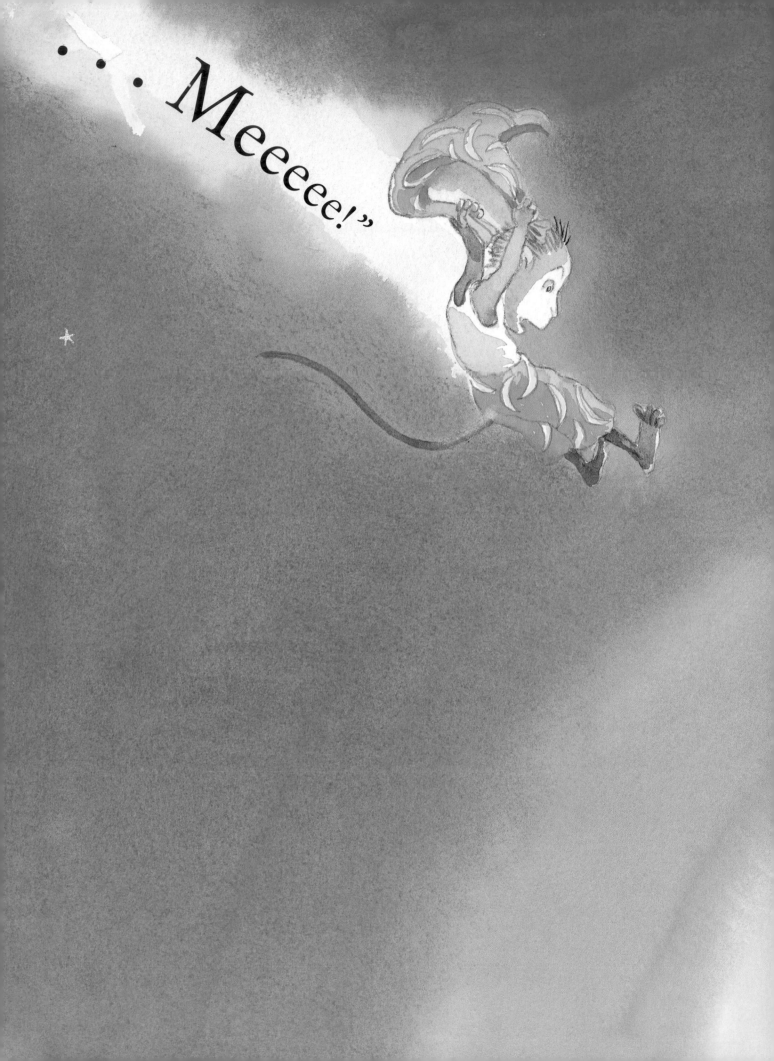

"HARRAH! HARROOO!

Now we'll get you —
and we're going to . . .

TICKLE YOU!!!"

TICKLE!
TICKLE!
TICKLE!
TICKLE!
TICKLE!

CAN'T CATCH . . .

"There, I've got you, safe and sound!
Come on, Little Monkey,
time for bed . . .

Good night, sleep tight.
Sweet Dreams."